A JOURNEY
TO THE CENTER OF THE
EARTH

Library of Congress Cataloging-in-Publication Data

James, Raymond.
   A journey to the center of the earth.

   (Troll illustrated classics)
   Summary: A team of explorers makes an expedition into
a crater in Iceland which leads to the center of the
earth and to incredible and horrifying discoveries.
    [1. Science fiction]   I. Verne, Jules, 1828-1905.
Journey to the center of the earth.   II. Geehan,
Wayne, ill.   III. Title.
PZ7.J1543Jo   1990   [Fic]   89-20560
ISBN 0-8167-1867-9 (lib. bdg.)
ISBN 0-8167-1868-7 (pbk.)

A JOURNEY TO THE CENTER OF THE EARTH

JULES VERNE

Retold by
Raymond James

Illustrated by
Wayne Geehan

Troll Associates

Get ready, Harry, for the adventure of a lifetime! The names of Von Hardwigg, Harry Lawson, and Hans Bjelke will be written in history!''

My uncle, Professor Von Hardwigg, was standing on the lip of a huge crater between the twin peaks of Mount Sneffels. This mountain on Iceland's western coast was really a volcano that had been inactive for centuries. We had traveled many hard miles, by railroad and ship and on foot, to reach Mount Sneffels.

Just a few weeks earlier, in Hamburg, Germany, my uncle and I had cracked the code of Arne Saknussemm's note. Written three hundred years ago, it told of the famed scientist's journey to the very center of the earth. And we intended to follow in Saknussemm's footsteps.

Our first task was to climb down into the crater. Then we'd have to wait below for the shadow of the southern peak to fall at high noon. Only during these last few days in June would the shadow point out the exact route Arne Saknussemm had taken so long ago.

"Ready, Hans?" the professor asked our guide. A native Icelander, Hans Bjelke was a tall, strapping hunter hired by my uncle. We knew we could depend on him in whatever lay ahead.

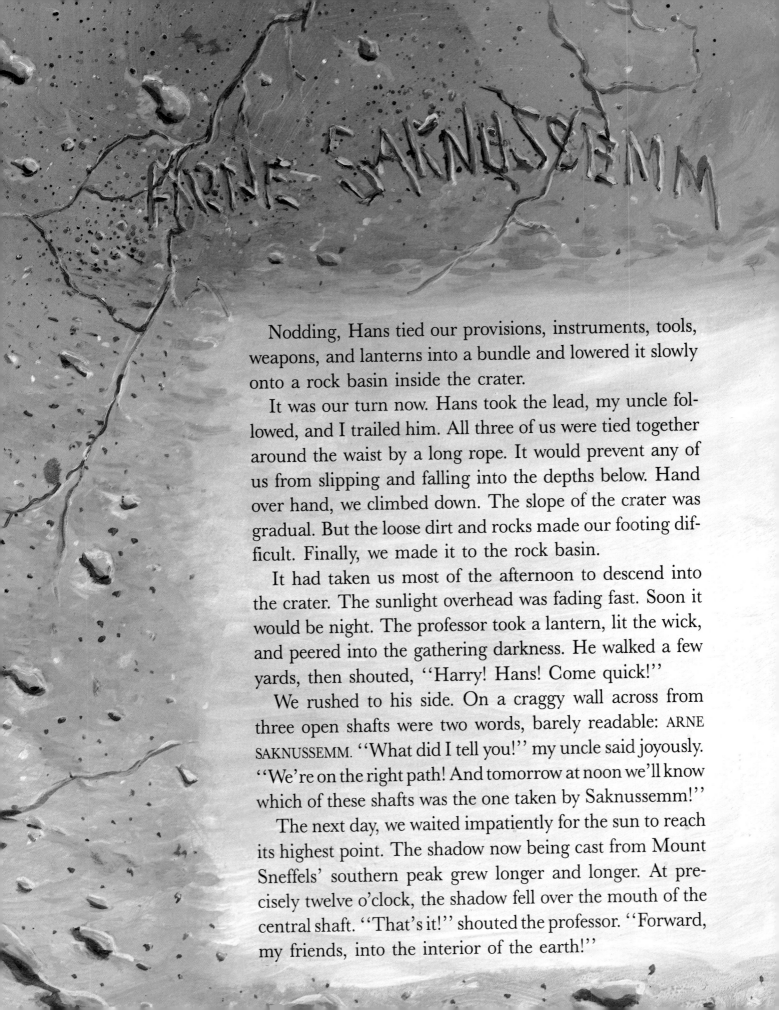

Nodding, Hans tied our provisions, instruments, tools, weapons, and lanterns into a bundle and lowered it slowly onto a rock basin inside the crater.

It was our turn now. Hans took the lead, my uncle followed, and I trailed him. All three of us were tied together around the waist by a long rope. It would prevent any of us from slipping and falling into the depths below. Hand over hand, we climbed down. The slope of the crater was gradual. But the loose dirt and rocks made our footing difficult. Finally, we made it to the rock basin.

It had taken us most of the afternoon to descend into the crater. The sunlight overhead was fading fast. Soon it would be night. The professor took a lantern, lit the wick, and peered into the gathering darkness. He walked a few yards, then shouted, ''Harry! Hans! Come quick!''

We rushed to his side. On a craggy wall across from three open shafts were two words, barely readable: ARNE SAKNUSSEMM. ''What did I tell you!'' my uncle said joyously. ''We're on the right path! And tomorrow at noon we'll know which of these shafts was the one taken by Saknussemm!''

The next day, we waited impatiently for the sun to reach its highest point. The shadow now being cast from Mount Sneffels' southern peak grew longer and longer. At precisely twelve o'clock, the shadow fell over the mouth of the central shaft. ''That's it!'' shouted the professor. ''Forward, my friends, into the interior of the earth!''

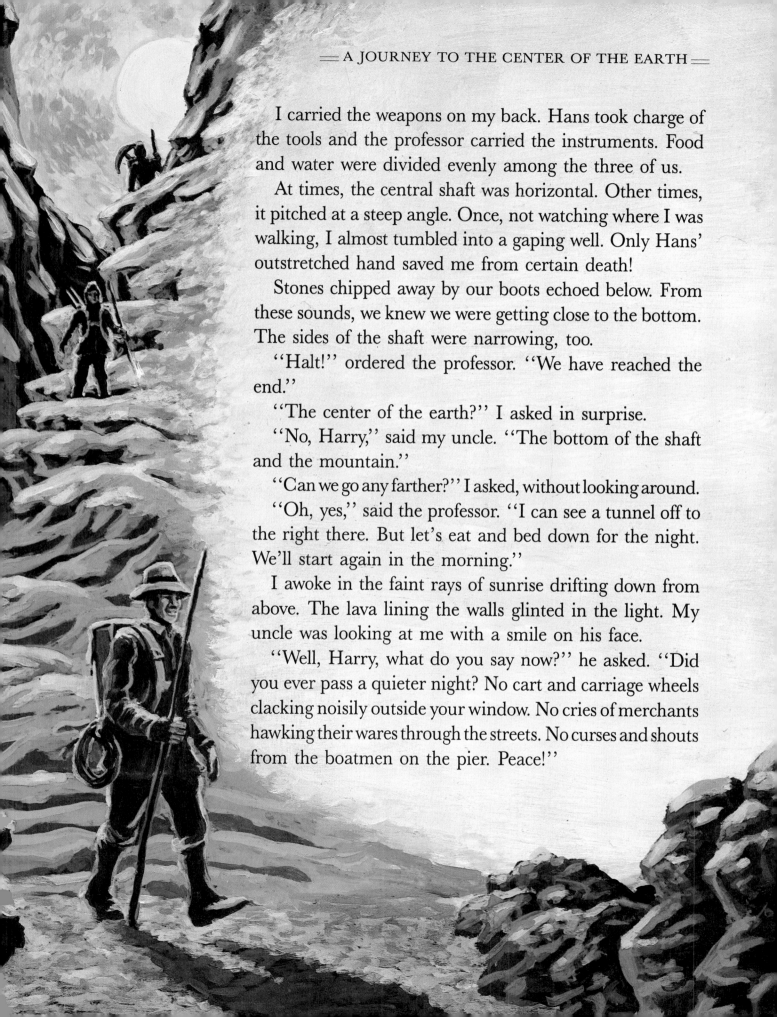

I carried the weapons on my back. Hans took charge of the tools and the professor carried the instruments. Food and water were divided evenly among the three of us.

At times, the central shaft was horizontal. Other times, it pitched at a steep angle. Once, not watching where I was walking, I almost tumbled into a gaping well. Only Hans' outstretched hand saved me from certain death!

Stones chipped away by our boots echoed below. From these sounds, we knew we were getting close to the bottom. The sides of the shaft were narrowing, too.

"Halt!" ordered the professor. "We have reached the end."

"The center of the earth?" I asked in surprise.

"No, Harry," said my uncle. "The bottom of the shaft and the mountain."

"Can we go any farther?" I asked, without looking around.

"Oh, yes," said the professor. "I can see a tunnel off to the right there. But let's eat and bed down for the night. We'll start again in the morning."

I awoke in the faint rays of sunrise drifting down from above. The lava lining the walls glinted in the light. My uncle was looking at me with a smile on his face.

"Well, Harry, what do you say now?" he asked. "Did you ever pass a quieter night? No cart and carriage wheels clacking noisily outside your window. No cries of merchants hawking their wares through the streets. No curses and shouts from the boatmen on the pier. Peace!"

"It *is* peaceful down here, Uncle," I said, wiping the sleep from my eyes. "But there's something eerie about all this quiet."

"Come, come, Harry," said the professor. "We've hardly begun. We've only made it to sea level. Our real journey starts now—actually *into* the earth itself!"

After a quick breakfast, I packed up my gear. Hans once more led the way, with my uncle and me following behind him. Each of us carried a lantern to light our way. We were now entering that level of the earth where night is eternal.

The tunnel we were traveling through was all aglow from the light of our lanterns. Huge formations of quartz and crystals hung from the roof and protruded from the ground. They were dazzling, and at times we had to shield our eyes as we walked.

"Magnificent! Glorious!" I said.

"Ah, Harry," said my uncle, "this is nothing compared to what we're likely to see later. Onward, my boy, onward!"

Hour after hour we advanced. The pace was steady but tiring. Then, the tunnel widened into a cavern. There was a fresh breeze wafting through it. But I couldn't locate its origin. That did not concern me as much as our rapidly dwindling water supply did.

"Professor," I said as we rested on some nearby rocks, "our water is now half gone. At this rate, we won't have enough to finish the journey. It'll last five more days—no more."

"Don't worry, Harry," said my uncle. "Soon we'll have plenty of water."

"From where, Professor?" I asked, unconvinced.

"Springs, Harry. Freshwater springs. They should be just underneath this crust of lava we've been walking through."

"How far would you say we've descended, Uncle?"

"I'm quite sure we're at least ten thousand feet below sea level," he replied.

Can it be possible? I wondered. We were already six thousand feet deeper in the earth than any other man had been before—except Arne Saknussemm.

"This is as good a place to sleep as any," said my uncle. "We'll resume in the morning."

Morning? I thought. It was hard to tell morning from night now. Only our pocket watches, lit by our lanterns, told us what period of the day it was. Otherwise, the darkness closed around us like a tomb. And it *was* a kind of tomb. Millions of tons of stone and dirt lay over me. I now knew what it must be like to be buried alive!

The next day was Tuesday, July 2. Right after breakfast, we continued our journey. Hans, taking the lead again, had gone ahead of us. My uncle and I could see his lantern swinging in the distance. But after a few hours, we caught up to Hans. All three of us were now standing at the crossroads of four tunnels. We had already walked down one. But which of the other three should we take?

"The eastern tunnel," said my uncle, consulting his compass.

The eastern tunnel dropped down gradually. It wound around immense rock formations and through naturally made stone arches. After a while, I could feel heat tingling along my face and hands. I also caught a strong whiff of smoke from what I assumed was boiling lava somewhere. I shuddered to think what would happen if bubbling, molten rock suddenly came up the tunnel.

But the scent of smoke and lava soon disappeared. The tunnel tapered off now. We were walking on a level, even upward plane. Were we heading back to the surface? Was my uncle wrong in choosing the eastern tunnel? These questions began to gnaw at me.

"Uncle?" I asked.

"Yes, Harry, what is it?"

"Are we going in the right direction?"

"I'm not sure, Harry," said the professor. "And I won't know until we reach the end of this tunnel."

"Our water's nearly gone," I said somberly.

"Then we'll have to ration it," said my uncle. Not once did he slacken his pace. He seemed determined to go on no matter what the hardships might be. But suffering from thirst and getting lost were two hardships the professor hadn't quite expected.

We walked on. In places where the tunnel narrowed, I touched the walls for support. Once, in pulling back my hand, I saw that it was black. "A coal mine!" I cried.

"A coal mine without miners," added my uncle. He was becoming more restless by the hour. We were down to our last half gourd of fresh water.

Then, we stopped. In front of us was a wall. Right, left, above, and below were also blocked. I stood there speechless. There was nowhere to go but back.

"Well," said the professor with a sigh, "at least we know this is *not* the road taken by Saknussemm. We'll have to return to the point where the four tunnels divide and choose another. Let's get some sleep here. Tomorrow's soon enough to start back."

I slept fitfully that night. Dreams of cool, clear water washed over me. I would have traded all the precious gems in the earth for one glass of pure spring water.

The next day, we departed at an early hour. There was no time to lose. We had to find water—and soon. The trip back was harder than the trip forward. Fatigue came quicker and crueler. My lips cracked and swelled from dryness. I was breathing heavily through my mouth. Often I had to stop and catch my breath. Then, as I approached the tunnel crossroads, I felt dizzy. The last thing I remember was the sound of my lantern falling to the ground.

"Drink!" I heard someone say.

Though still lightheaded, I felt cool water pouring into my parched mouth. It was my uncle! He was giving me his last swallow in the gourd. It wasn't much, but it revived me.

"My dear uncle," I said gratefully. Tears rolled down my cheeks.

"There, there, Harry," he said soothingly. "You rest a while. You'll need your strength to continue."

"Continue?" I said in a loud voice. "Surely, Uncle, you'll agree we must return to the surface immediately. Our water is gone. We must go back!"

"Absolutely not," replied the professor. "If you feel you must go back, then do so. Take Hans with you. *I will go on alone!*"

13

The idea of abandoning my uncle in the dark depths of the earth was too terrible to think about. "All right, Uncle," I said. "All right. We'll go on. But promise me that if we don't find water by tomorrow, we'll return to the surface."

"I promise, Harry," he said. "And I think we'll find water in the western tunnel. After you passed out, I did a little exploring. The western tunnel goes straight down. We should find springs there."

The western tunnel was streaked with copper, manganese, and traces of platinum and gold. Despite the beauty of these ores, I was miserable. We still hadn't found water. And I was getting weaker all the time. I slowed to the point where both Hans and the professor were far ahead of me. I couldn't keep up. Once more, I fell unconscious.

"Harry," a voice spoke. "Harry!"

When I opened my eyes, I saw my uncle's face peering down at me. Off to the side, I saw Hans leaving. "Come back, Hans!" I yelled. "Don't leave us! We *must* stay together!" But he ignored my plea. His lantern became a faint glow, then disappeared in the darkness.

"Oh, Uncle, what's to become of us?" I asked, my heart sinking.

"*Shhh,* Harry. Rest now."

Only a few hours had gone by when I heard footsteps approaching from the darkness. Hans was returning! He went over to the professor and said, "Water."

"What?" blurted my uncle.

"Water! Water!" I shouted, clapping my hands. "Lead the way, Hans!" Tired and weak as I was, the thought of fresh water nearby got me to my feet.

Nipping at Hans' heels, my uncle and I followed our guide farther down the tunnel. We must have traveled three thousand feet forward and at least two thousand feet downward. Then, I heard it—the sound of rushing water. But where? Apart from the dull roar, there was no sign of water anywhere.

"A torrent!" exclaimed my uncle. "Flowing beside us!"

Hans put his ear against the wall of the tunnel. He inched along, then stopped. He was at the spot where the sound of the water was loudest. Perhaps less than two feet of granite separated us from it.

Hans took out a heavy crowbar and started swinging at the rock. Chip by chip, it fell away. Soon he had made a hole a foot deep. He swung again. This time, there was a loud hiss. Then, a jet of water gushed through the hole in the rock and struck the opposite wall.

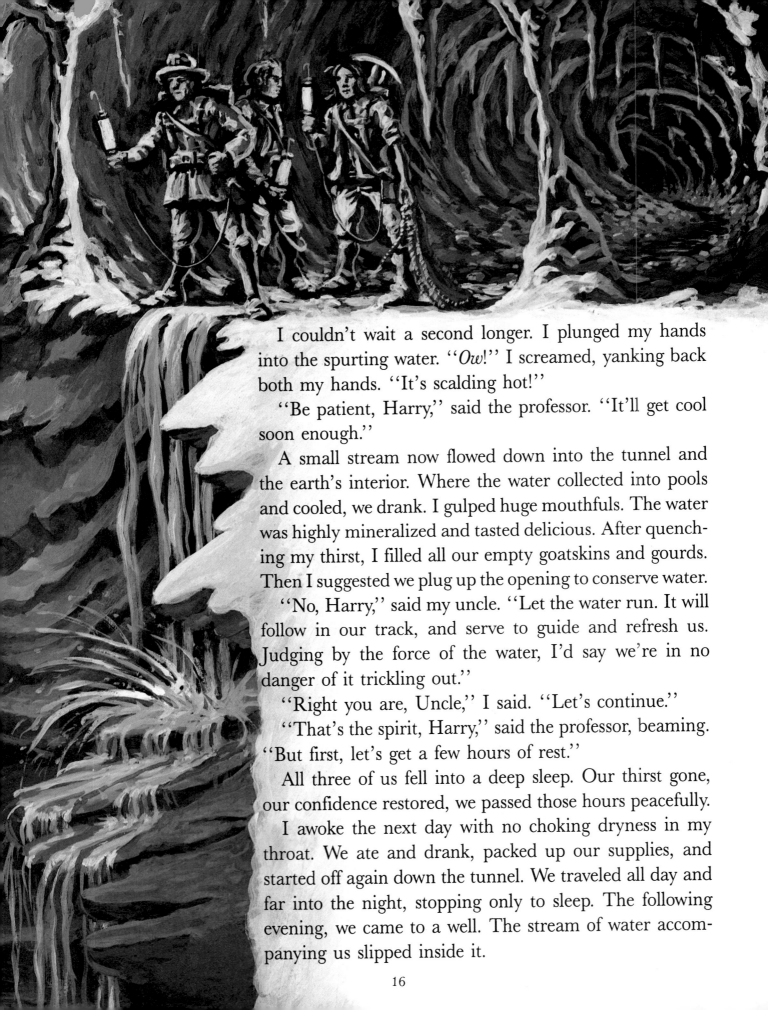

I couldn't wait a second longer. I plunged my hands into the spurting water. "*Ow!*" I screamed, yanking back both my hands. "It's scalding hot!"

"Be patient, Harry," said the professor. "It'll get cool soon enough."

A small stream now flowed down into the tunnel and the earth's interior. Where the water collected into pools and cooled, we drank. I gulped huge mouthfuls. The water was highly mineralized and tasted delicious. After quenching my thirst, I filled all our empty goatskins and gourds. Then I suggested we plug up the opening to conserve water.

"No, Harry," said my uncle. "Let the water run. It will follow in our track, and serve to guide and refresh us. Judging by the force of the water, I'd say we're in no danger of it trickling out."

"Right you are, Uncle," I said. "Let's continue."

"That's the spirit, Harry," said the professor, beaming. "But first, let's get a few hours of rest."

All three of us fell into a deep sleep. Our thirst gone, our confidence restored, we passed those hours peacefully.

I awoke the next day with no choking dryness in my throat. We ate and drank, packed up our supplies, and started off again down the tunnel. We traveled all day and far into the night, stopping only to sleep. The following evening, we came to a well. The stream of water accompanying us slipped inside it.

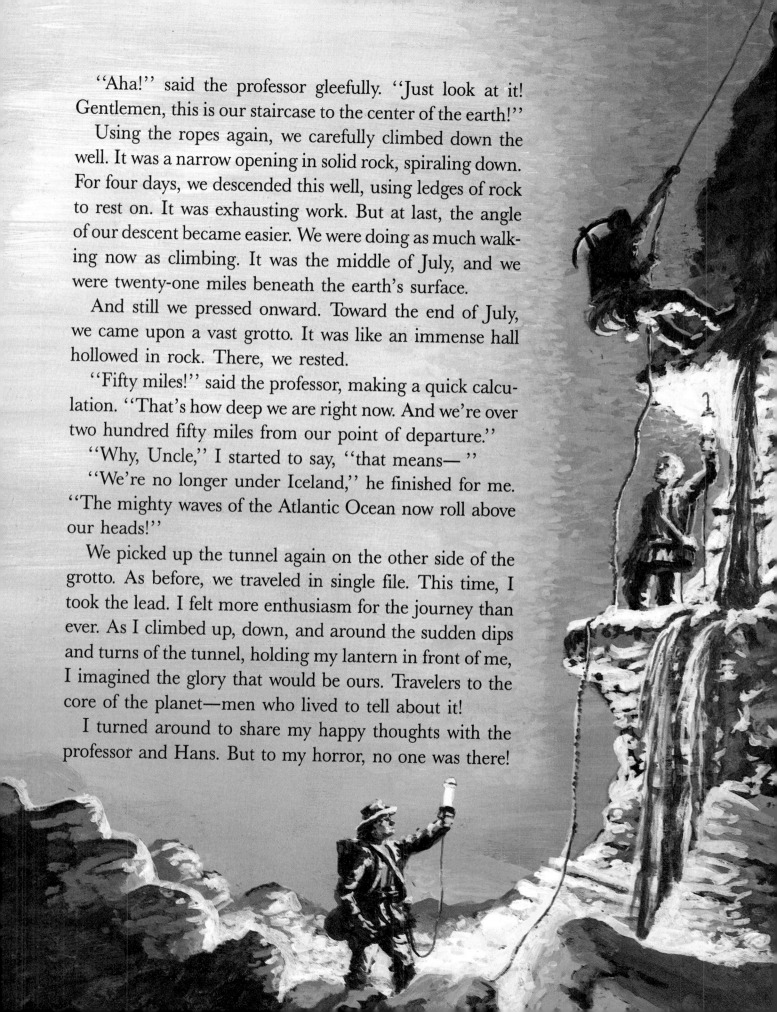

"Aha!" said the professor gleefully. "Just look at it! Gentlemen, this is our staircase to the center of the earth!"

Using the ropes again, we carefully climbed down the well. It was a narrow opening in solid rock, spiraling down. For four days, we descended this well, using ledges of rock to rest on. It was exhausting work. But at last, the angle of our descent became easier. We were doing as much walking now as climbing. It was the middle of July, and we were twenty-one miles beneath the earth's surface.

And still we pressed onward. Toward the end of July, we came upon a vast grotto. It was like an immense hall hollowed in rock. There, we rested.

"Fifty miles!" said the professor, making a quick calculation. "That's how deep we are right now. And we're over two hundred fifty miles from our point of departure."

"Why, Uncle," I started to say, "that means— "

"We're no longer under Iceland," he finished for me. "The mighty waves of the Atlantic Ocean now roll above our heads!"

We picked up the tunnel again on the other side of the grotto. As before, we traveled in single file. This time, I took the lead. I felt more enthusiasm for the journey than ever. As I climbed up, down, and around the sudden dips and turns of the tunnel, holding my lantern in front of me, I imagined the glory that would be ours. Travelers to the core of the planet—men who lived to tell about it!

I turned around to share my happy thoughts with the professor and Hans. But to my horror, no one was there!

Well, I thought, I've obviously been walking too fast. Or my uncle and Hans stopped to rest farther back. Either way, I only had to retrace my steps and join them.

For a quarter of an hour, I walked. I looked everywhere—front, back, and to both sides. Not a living soul! I called out. Only my echo answered me. A cold shiver ripped through me. My skin broke out in a clammy sweat. Stay calm, I told myself silently. You'll find them. They *can't* be far behind.

I walked on for another hour. A deathly silence engulfed me. The only sound was that of my footsteps, though I swore I could hear my heart pounding inside me. Then I thought of the stream of water coursing through the tunnel. That would lead me back to my companions! I reached down and felt for the stream. My hands touched nothing but hard, dry granite. The stream I depended on had disappeared completely!

The panic I felt before became like a fever. The absence of the stream proved that I had taken a wrong turn. But where was I? Could I be—oh, please, no—*lost*? "Uncle!" I yelled at the top of my lungs. "Hans! HELP!" But again, only echoes replied, mocking me.

I raced forward. The lantern I held before me swung wildly. But I didn't care. I *had* to find the stream again, *had* to find the point where I had made a wrong turn. I stumbled, picked myself up, fell again, and got up again. My hands were bleeding. I also tasted blood in my mouth, cut by a sharp rock. Still, I ran. I ran until I was just a few feet shy of an enormous granite rock sealing off the tunnel. There was no way out!

I collapsed in misery onto the ground. The light in my lantern was flickering. I had damaged it during one of my falls. I looked on that pale, waning light as my life. If it died, would I? The flame shrunk until it was almost a red spark. Then, *poof*! It was gone. I was in total darkness.

Leaning against the tunnel wall, I thought my ears were playing tricks on me. I heard a prolonged rumbling sound from a distance. Voices? I wondered. It was too much to hope for. But still, the sound persisted. Then, I could plainly make out *two* muffled voices far off in the expanse of blackness.

"Help!" I shouted, trying to make my voice carry along the tunnel wall. "Help! I'm dying!"

I waited for what seemed an eternity. Then, a voice came traveling back along the wall to me. "Harry, my boy, is that you?"

"Yes, Uncle," I replied as loudly as I could. "YES!"

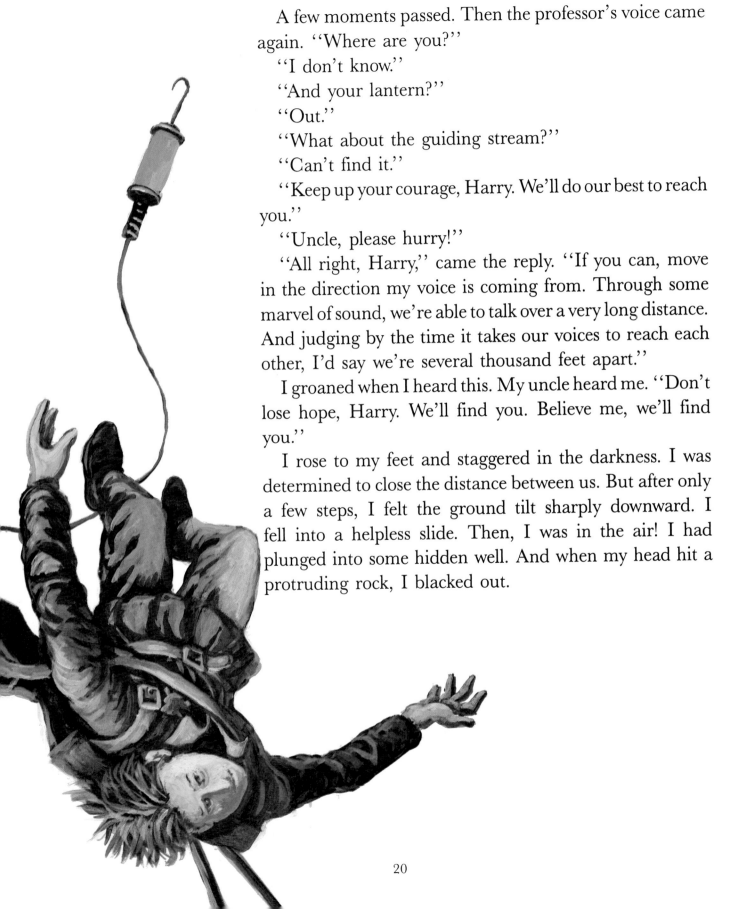

A few moments passed. Then the professor's voice came again. "Where are you?"

"I don't know."

"And your lantern?"

"Out."

"What about the guiding stream?"

"Can't find it."

"Keep up your courage, Harry. We'll do our best to reach you."

"Uncle, please hurry!"

"All right, Harry," came the reply. "If you can, move in the direction my voice is coming from. Through some marvel of sound, we're able to talk over a very long distance. And judging by the time it takes our voices to reach each other, I'd say we're several thousand feet apart."

I groaned when I heard this. My uncle heard me. "Don't lose hope, Harry. We'll find you. Believe me, we'll find you."

I rose to my feet and staggered in the darkness. I was determined to close the distance between us. But after only a few steps, I felt the ground tilt sharply downward. I fell into a helpless slide. Then, I was in the air! I had plunged into some hidden well. And when my head hit a protruding rock, I blacked out.

The first thing I saw when I opened my eyes again was the face of my uncle. He was leaning over me. There was a tear in his eye as he cried, "He lives! He lives!"

"Hello, Uncle," I said feebly. My head was swimming. "How...long was I unconscious?"

"Four days," he replied, wiping my mouth with his handkerchief.

"Four days!" I exclaimed hoarsely. "What happened? All I can recall is falling, then hitting my head-- " I reached up immediately to touch my forehead. It was wrapped in a bandage. A sharp, stinging pain told me I hadn't completely recovered.

"Eat first," urged the professor. "Then we'll talk about how we found you."

I was very hungry and devoured every morsel of food put before me. It was then I noticed something very odd. There was light everywhere—light *not* cast by the lanterns. And I could hear the murmur of waves and the rustling of wind. Where *was* I?

"Feeling better?" asked my uncle. I nodded, then he continued. "Though you may not think so now, Harry, your fall was a lucky one. Our own path to you was cut off by a boulder. So Hans and I had to go down a side tunnel and hope to come back up farther on. Imagine our surprise, then, when our lanterns showed *you* lying directly in our path. It's a miracle!"

"Dear uncle," I said, "let us take care never to separate again."

The professor nodded. Then he saw the confused look on my face. "What is it, Harry?"

"Am I in my right mind?"

"I should think so, Harry. You took a nasty blow to the head, but that's healing quite nicely now. Why do you ask?"

"Because I believe we've returned to the surface of Mother Earth."

"No, Harry," said my uncle. "We haven't."

"Then how do you explain this light? This wind I feel? These waves I hear?"

"Rather than try to explain that which I can't," answered my uncle, "I'll let you see for yourself. Come with me, Harry. And be careful in the open air."

"Open air?"

"Yes, Harry. I have to warn you that the wind can be quite violent. When it slackens a bit, we should be able to board and head out to sea."

Board? Sea? I was beginning to wonder if my uncle hadn't received a sharp rap on *his* head. For the life of me, I couldn't understand what he was talking about.

"Just follow me," he said, walking through a passageway that led to a vast stretch of blue.

"A sea!" I cried out.

"Yes, Harry, an underground sea," said the professor.

We were both standing on a beach, looking out on water that seemed endless. The sand was soft and golden, mixed with small shells. Spray blew in my face as the surf crashed on the shore. This was more than a sea—it was an ocean!

"There's something electric in the air, Harry, that gives off all this light," said my uncle. "It's the only explanation I can come up with. And this sea and the tremendous vault of rock overhead could have been formed during some bygone age. Now I know how Arne Saknussemm must have felt when he was standing here."

The air, gusty as it was, felt clean and fresh in my lungs. And the bright light cheered me. After spending fifty days in tunnels of darkness, I was happy to be around waves, wind, and radiant light again.

"Care to explore a little with me?" my uncle asked me.

"Sure," I replied, my head spinning from the sights surrounding me. "Where's Hans?"

"Finishing the raft we'll be using to cross this sea," answered my uncle. "Come on."

"But where did he get the wood for the raft?"

"You'll see," said the professor. "You'll see."

We walked hundreds of yards along the shoreline. Just past a mound of large rocks, we found ourselves close to a forest. It was full of trees with straight trunks and tufted tops shaped like thick umbrellas. I racked my brain for a clue. What could grow that huge?

"Mushrooms," said my uncle matter-of-factly. "A forest of gigantic mushrooms."

I couldn't believe it. Here were white mushrooms standing nearly forty feet tall, with tops nearly half as wide! They grew by the thousands. And farther on I saw grasses as tall as ferns, and ferns as tall as pine trees!

"Amazing, Harry, isn't it?"

"Yes, Professor," I mumbled in astonishment. "Why, one would swear we were back in some ancient, primitive age."

"You may be right, Harry. Certainly, the size of these plants suggests as much. And where there are plants as lush and large as these, there are bound to be animals."

"What makes you say that, Professor?" I asked in alarm.

"Take a good look under your feet, Harry," he replied.

I gazed down, squinting in the light reflected from the sand. The professor was right. I could now see the sunken contours of hundreds of bones. Some were as big as tree trunks!

"What kinds of animals could— "

" —leave bones as big as these?" interrupted my uncle. "That's been puzzling me ever since Hans and I stumbled onto this beach. But I'm not sure."

By the time we returned back down the beach, Hans had finished the raft. It was made from fossil wood he had collected inland. About ten feet long and five feet wide, the raft was strongly built. Its thick beams were lashed tightly together with heavy ropes. My doubts about whether the raft would float were quickly put to rest when Hans pulled it into the water. The raft bobbed proudly between the waves.

The three of us settled down to our evening meal. Afterward, Hans built a small fire. The flames crackled brightly. They comforted me as I drifted off to sleep. Who knew what strange beasts might be lurking about?

It was now the middle of August. We rose early, doused the fire, and put all our supplies on board the raft. Hans had made a mast from two long pieces of wood, which he tied together for extra strength. A sail was cut from a linen sheet and slung along the mast. And a crude rudder was fashioned from driftwood. We were now ready for our sea voyage.

The wind blew hard, and our sail pulled the raft at a blistering speed. Ahead of us was nothing but water. It seemed to have no limit. Soon we passed through large clumps of seaweed just below the surface. Some of the strands were hundreds of feet long.

After a few hours, Hans pulled out a line and hook. He baited the hook with a small piece of meat, then dropped it over the side. Minutes passed, then there came a sudden tug on his line. Hans pulled it up carefully. Dangling on the hook was a fish, struggling for its life.

''A sturgeon!'' I cried out.

''Yes, it's of the sturgeon family, all right,'' said the professor. ''But definitely not of our time. This fish has been extinct for ages. Still, it shall make a fine meal.''

In two hours, Hans had caught a large number of the fish. We salted and stored them away for future meals. All three of us felt content. Our backs were to the wind, which remained strong and steady. My uncle scanned the horizon with his telescope. But as the hours slipped by, his smile became a frown.

"What's the matter, Uncle?" I asked. "We're moving at a very rapid rate, no?"

"I'm not so much concerned about how fast we're going, Harry," he said, "as *where* we're going. This sea is much greater than I expected."

"But if we're following the route taken by Saknussemm, we can't be going wrong."

"That's precisely the question, Harry," said my uncle. "*Are* we following the path of Saknussemm? *Did* he cross this large body of water?"

The professor raised the telescope to his eye again and peered out. I leaned against the mast. His worry was now mine. The raft skimmed the waves rapidly. We *were* making excellent progress, but to where? No land was in sight.

My uncle put down his telescope, then tied a crowbar to a length of rope and dropped it overboard to take some soundings of the sea's depth. But he had trouble hoisting the crowbar back up. Finally, a tremendous heave brought it on board. All of us examined it. The crowbar looked as if it had been crushed between two very hard substances.

Hans whispered something into the professor's ear. My uncle nodded. "What?" I asked.

"Teeth, Harry," the professor said grimly. "Teeth."

The constant light on the sea made it as hard to tell day from night as the constant darkness in the tunnels had. But I knew we had spent many days on the raft.

One night, as I slumbered by the mast, I felt a sudden, awful shock. I awoke with a start, thinking we had struck a sunken rock. Then I felt the raft being lifted out of the water. No sooner were we in the air than we hit the water with a loud slap.

"Look!" said Hans, pointing ahead of the raft. About two hundred yards in front of us was a huge black mass moving up and down.

"It's a sea monster!" I shouted in terror.

"Yes," cried my uncle, equally stunned at the sight. "And over there is a mammoth sea lizard!"

I looked over to where he was pointing. Then I saw something else. "A crocodile!" I yelled. "And look at the size of its teeth and jaws!"

"A whale!" said the professor. "I can see her enormous flippers. See how she blows air and water!" Just then, a torrent of water shot up from the creature and rose a hundred feet into the air.

We were surrounded by monsters of the deep. They were of nearly supernatural size and shape. The smallest of them could have easily crushed our raft and ourselves with one bite. They swirled around us. Hans pulled hard at the rudder, trying to steer us clear of them. But it was no use. They followed every twist and turn we made.

Then, it grew strangely quiet. All the creatures had submerged. I looked at my uncle. He glanced at Hans, and Hans eyed me. What was happening? All three of us turned our gaze to the water. There was no sign of movement, of any life below.

"*Whew!*" I finally said, wiping my forehead with the back of my hand. "That was too close for comf—"

I never got the last word out. For at that instant, two mighty sea creatures rose to the surface with a fury. They rushed right at each other. The pair were no more than a few hundred feet in front of us.

"Uncle, what in the name of—"

"Brace yourself, Harry," said the professor, cutting me off. "You are witnessing something no living man has ever seen, something truly incredible. The creature on the left is one of the most feared sea reptiles that ever lived— Ichthyosaurus. The creature on the right is another tyrant of the sea—Plesiosaurus."

"Dinosaurs!" I gasped, eyes widening. "Real live dinosaurs!"

Never have I seen a fiercer, more terrifying struggle. The two giant creatures attacked each other over and over again. The sea around them churned violently. Blood stained the surface. Snarls and screams and the sounds of flesh tearing and bones snapping filled the air. It was a nightmare come alive!

One hour, two hours, three hours passed, and still they fought on. The long neck of the Plesiosaurus was flowing red. One of its eyes dangled. A fin from the back of the Ichthyosaurus had been ripped off. And a deep, ugly gouge in its side was pouring blood like a faucet. Every ounce of strength was being used by one dinosaur to destroy the other.

Suddenly, each of them had the other in its jaws. In this horrifying death grip, the two disappeared below the water's surface. The force of their descent created a whirlpool that nearly sucked the raft down with them.

Several minutes went by. Was this awful combat to end below, out of our sight? I didn't have to wonder for long. Up popped the torn, tattered head of the Plesiosaurus. It thrashed the waves with its bleeding neck. White foam and dark red blood oozed from its mouth. The eye that dangled earlier had been shorn off. Clearly, this snake-necked dinosaur was in the last agony of death.

Closer and closer to the raft came the dying Plesiosaurus. We could now see that its neck had been almost completely bitten through. With one last shiver that sent a chill through my own body, the neck of the Plesiosaurus plopped into the water beside us. It floated aimlessly. The remaining eye of the dinosaur was open and glassy. It was dead.

As for the Ichthyosaurus, it never resurfaced. And Hans had no intention of waiting for its return. He grabbed hold of the rudder and steered us swiftly away. The wind, strong as always, filled our sail. We were all relieved to have that maddening death struggle far behind us.

"We made it, Uncle!" I said happily. "For a while there, I thought *we'd* be their next meal. From here on, we should have clear sailing, don't you think? What could be worse than facing two sea monsters?"

"That!" said my uncle, pointing behind me.

I turned around. A low mass of dark clouds was moving straight toward us. But what really frightened me were the streaks of lightning and the flashes of fire rippling through the clouds.

"I fear we're in for some hard weather," said the professor.

"Hard weather?" I said in disbelief. "Uncle, that's one tremendous storm heading our way right now! And we're fully exposed on this raft!" I reached up to trim the sail.

"No, Harry!" ordered my uncle. Darkness had already fallen over the raft. "Let the storm do what it will. Only let me first see a glimmer of land. We must keep the sail up."

"But we'll be dashed to pieces," I said.

The professor was about to reply when the storm broke over our heads. Sheets of rain drenched us. Hailstones pelted us. The wind raged around us. Huge waves battered the raft. It was all my uncle and I could do to cling to the mast.

Hans held tightly to the rudder. The strain in his face and back showed he could barely keep the raft steady. The sail billowed wildly, filling out like a soap bubble about to burst. We were being whisked along at a speed impossible to guess. For a while, I thought we were flying over the whitecaps.

A sudden, deafening boom knocked me down on the raft. It was an enormous clap of thunder. My ears rang. Then lightning sizzled through the air, shedding its white-hot light for only a moment. The raft pitched and tossed on the waves. There were times when I could feel it whirling about, out of control. I looked over at Hans. He stood erect, still clutching the rudder, still trying to steer us through the storm.

"Uncle, are you all right?" I shouted. My voice seemed lost in the roar of thunder.

"Yes, Harry," he said, spitting out seawater. "Hold fast! This can't last forever!"

But to my mind, it did. What we experienced that first day of the storm was tame compared to the next three days. The darkness grew thicker, the thunder louder, the waves higher, and the wind and rain fiercer. During the whole time, we got no sleep. We gobbled pieces of salted fish to satisfy our hunger. Our arms ached from holding on so tightly for so long.

We managed to tie down our cargo, but much of it came loose from the pounding of the wind and the waves. We lost quite a few supplies, including all our weapons. And soon we had to lash each other down to the raft for fear that *we* would be next to go overboard.

Then, a powerful gust of wind snapped the mast and blew the sail up into the air like a kite. It vanished in the darkness. When I turned my eyes back to the foot of the raft, I froze in terror. For there, spinning at a fantastic rate, was a ball of fire!

Suddenly, it darted up, down, and around the raft. The fiery orb even singed the hairs standing up on my neck as it flew by what was left of the mast. Then it landed—right on our powder keg! I said a fast prayer, convinced we'd all be blown to kingdom come. But luckily, the keg didn't ignite.

All three of us now watched the burning ball rise above the powder keg and burst into a shower of fire. Tongues of flame licked at my body. I shook them off as best as I could. Some hissed into the sea. Then, all was darkness again.

''Uncle! Hans!'' These were the last words I spoke before we crashed. It all happened so quickly. The ropes binding me to the raft snapped like thread. I was knocked clean off the raft and into the water. Then I lost consciousness.

Vaguely, I had the sensation that the sea was bubbling over my face. But then, something took hold of me and lifted my head above the water. Somehow, I was being pulled, dragged really. I could feel sand scraping under my heels. On my face I felt a sharp pinging of water. Then I heard a voice.

''Open your eyes, Harry!''

I did as the voice instructed. It was my uncle, kneeling beside me. Hans was on my other side. I could see that the storm had lessened, becoming a steady downpour.

''You owe Hans here your life, Harry,'' said the professor. ''He grabbed you out of the waves in the nick of time. If not for him, you would have surely drowned.''

I clasped Hans' hand. ''Thank you, my friend. I won't forget this.''

"Not only did Hans save you, Harry," continued my uncle, "but he also saved a number of our supplies. He even salvaged what remains of our raft. The offshore rocks claimed the rest."

Hans smiled. Then both he and the professor helped me to my feet. We moved out of the rain and under an overhang of rocks on the beach. There, we waited out the storm.

It finally broke the next morning. The change was magical. A soft breeze blew in off the smooth surface of the water. Light shone down on sand and sea together. It was hard to believe that just yesterday a storm had nearly killed us.

The professor took out his compass to get a reading. Twice he shook it, each time grumbling. The third time, he just stood staring at the compass. I rushed over to his side and glanced at it. The needle was pointing due north—but in the direction we assumed was south! It was pointing to the shore, not to the sea.

Both of us stood there, blank-faced. The awful truth was sinking in—we were back where we started. After days at sea, eluding sea monsters, fighting a storm, we were no farther along than before. The storm had turned us around, dumping us back on the shore we had set out from.

"No, no, no!" I cried. "It can't be! Not after all we've been through!"

The professor looked at me sadly. "I'm afraid it's true, Harry." Then his lower lip quivered in anger. "But we're not beaten yet! Fate has played a terrible trick on us. But we're not through. Not by a long shot! We'll repair the raft, gather more provisions, and set out again."

"But Uncle— "

"No buts, Harry," he interrupted, waving off further argument. "This is just a setback. It is not defeat. I won't allow it!"

Never before had I seen my uncle so stubborn. He wouldn't listen to any objections at all. Hans was given the task of repairing the raft. The professor and I would explore the shoreline, which was north of the beach we had originally departed. Our job was to collect fresh water and pick whatever fruits we could find for food.

As my uncle and I trudged along the beach, we came upon a plain of bones. It looked like an immense cemetery. Here were the remains of hundreds of prehistoric animals. Then the professor picked up a skull that had a familiar shape.

"Harry, my boy, this is a human head!" he said, holding the skull in his hands. "And judging by its size, I'd say the skull belonged to someone who lived during the age of mastodons."

Extinct for centuries, mastodons were similar to elephants. They were huge, measuring fourteen feet at the shoulder, and had thick skin and tusks. Their trunks were long and powerful, able to rip stout branches from trees in their search for food.

We moved farther up the beach. Ahead of us now was a forest. This one was filled, not with mushrooms, but with huge palm, pine, yew, and cypress trees. When we got to the edge of the forest, we could see something stirring just a short distance inside. We made our way through the thick underbrush and around the trees. I stopped short, grabbing my uncle by his arm.

Before us was a whole herd of mastodons! Not fossils, not bones, but living, breathing mastodons! They were tearing down large boughs from the trees with their trunks. Smaller trees they uprooted with their tusks. Masses of green leaves and slender, leafy branches were being devoured by the beasts.

"Will wonders never cease, Uncle?" I said, staring at the creatures.

"No, Harry, they won't," replied the professor, looking off to the side of the mastodons.

There, holding a branch and watching the herd, was a giant man! He was over twelve feet tall, with a head as big and shaggy as a buffalo's. I could only conclude that he was the keeper of this mastodon herd.

"Come, Uncle," I said, leading him away by the arm. "We must get out of here before that giant picks up our scent. Remember, we have no weapons."

As we hurried back down to where Hans was fixing the raft, I saw something jutting out of the sand near some rocks. I slowed my pace and walked over to it. Brushing away some sand, I picked the object up.

"What is it, Harry?" asked the professor.

I held up a rusty dagger.

"*Hmm*," said my uncle, taking the dagger from me and examining it. "It's made of steel, so it couldn't have come from any native creature here. I'd guess it to be from the sixteenth century. Just look at the design. And the edge seems to have been blunted from...from...oh, Harry, I've *got* it!"

"Got what?"

"The dagger must have been used to carve something into the rocks here. But what? Quick, Harry! Search every rock face here. I feel we're on the verge of an important discovery!"

I did as the professor told me. Together, we looked high and low. Then, in a spot where the shore became extremely narrow and the sea seeped into the sand, I found an opening in the rocks. It was the entrance to a dark and gloomy tunnel. And on a granite wall were carved two initials: A.S.

"Arne Saknussemm!" my uncle and I blurted out at the same time.

Hans, the professor, and I wasted no time in starting down the tunnel. As we walked, I thought what a strange twist of fate brought us here. The storm we had cursed earlier put us on the right path. Without that storm, we may never have returned to this shore and found the route Saknussemm took.

"Five thousand more miles," said the professor, as if they were a hop, skip, and jump from here. "That's all there is to the center of the earth!"

But then Hans stopped in front of us. A huge stone completely blocked the tunnel.

"I don't believe it!" I said, groaning. "How can this be?"

"Good point, Harry," said the professor, examining the stone. "This couldn't have been here when Saknussemm came through. It must have shifted or rolled in place many years afterward."

"What should we do, Uncle?" I asked.

"Blast, Harry!" the professor said, turning around and walking back out of the tunnel. "We'll blast the stone with the gunpowder we have. I'm not going to let this oversized pebble stop me. Come on! Let's bring the raft up."

We brought the newly repaired raft to a spot just offshore from the tunnel entrance. Then Hans and I went back into the tunnel with pickaxes. We bored a hole large enough to pack in the gunpowder. Our fuse was a trail of gunpowder. Hans went back out of the tunnel to join the professor by the raft. They were waiting for me to light the fuse.

"Let her go, Harry!" shouted my uncle from the beach. "We're ready!"

With that, I lit the fuse and ran out of the tunnel. Then all three of us scrambled onto the raft. Hans expertly guided it out to a safe distance. Seconds passed. We watched the tunnel entrance, waiting for the explosion.

KA-BOOM!

The blast was more powerful than we expected. Large chunks of rock flew everywhere. A cloud of smoke and dust funneled into the sky. Then the sand leading into the tunnel caved in, falling below the waterline.

The sea in front of us rose up under the force of the explosion. It lifted the raft high into the air and just as quickly dropped us. As we glided down the last big wave, I could see the tunnel gaping wide before us. The sea was rushing into it. And the raft, with us on board, was hurtling toward the foaming mouth.

"Uncle! Hans!" I shouted, frightened out of my wits.

I had no time to say more. We were plunged into the tunnel. Darkness swallowed us. The raft was being carried along at a dizzying speed through the blackness. All three of us held onto the mast for dear life. Time and again, the seething water rammed the raft against the craggy sides of the tunnel. We were helpless!

"Harry, are you all right?" asked my uncle through the gloom.

"Yes, Uncle," I replied. My knuckles were already stiff from gripping the mast. "How about Hans?"

"He's okay," the professor replied. Then fear crept into his voice. "This descent may get worse before it gets better."

Within moments, my uncle's words came true. The raft dropped sharply downward. Water gushed over me. It spluttered from my mouth and nose and stung my eyes. We fell for what seemed hours.

Suddenly, the raft splashed into a deep pool and plunged underwater. I held my breath and held on. Then, when my lungs were about to burst, the raft eased to the surface. I could hear the professor and Hans gagging near me as they tried to clear their lungs of seawater. It was then that I felt the raft start to rise.

"Uncle, am I dreaming or are we moving upward?"

"You're not dreaming, Harry," he said, disappointed. "Unless I miss my guess, we are now being thrust up a volcanic shaft. I'd give anything for a lantern right now!"

I saw a match strike. Hans was holding the small flame in his hand. He then tried to light the wick of the one lantern not lost during the fall down the tunnel. Though damp, the wick did catch eventually. We could now see each other.

"Well done, Hans!" said the professor. "Well done!"

"Uncle, is it getting warm in here?" I asked. I could feel heat slowly seeping into my sopping wet clothes.

"I noticed that, too, Harry," the professor answered. "I can only conclude that we're traveling up the shaft of an *active* volcano."

"You mean if we don't drown, get smashed like pancakes, or die of starvation, we can look forward to being burned alive?" I said, beginning to panic.

"Faith, Harry," said my uncle sternly. "Faith. While there's life, there's hope."

I reached out to touch the sides of the shaft.

"*Yow!*" I screamed, pulling my hand back. The shaft was red hot. And the steam hissing around the raft told me that the water pushing us upward was boiling. There could be no doubt about what was making the water boil—lava!

We were moving at a greater speed than ever. Peering upward, I said a quick prayer. But then I saw a speck of light from above. As we rushed upward, the light grew brighter. The professor and Hans were gazing at it, too. It could mean only one thing—sunlight. And sunlight meant we were heading toward the earth's surface!

"Hans, Harry, get ready!" shouted my uncle. "We are about to be pushed out of this shaft!"

Higher and higher we rose. The sunlight was bathing us now. I could even see tufts of clouds overhead. Then, like a cannon shot, we were fired into empty space. I felt weight-less, almost giddy in the air and blazing light. Then I passed out.

When I awoke, I found myself sprawled in some bushes growing on the side of the volcano. I glanced over at the professor and Hans. They were picking themselves out of the same scrub. If we hadn't fallen into these bushes, we surely would have broken our necks. The three of us were unharmed, apart from some scratches and bruises.

After plucking some nettles out of our clothes, we started down the volcano. Groves of olive and fig trees grew near the bottom. The weather was sunny and quite warm. We all knew wherever we were, it wasn't Iceland.

When we came upon some houses nestled below, we saw a man working in a garden. My uncle walked over to him and asked where we were. He tried German, then French, and finally Italian. The man answered in Italian. "Stromboli," he said. We were on an island just off the coast of Sicily. We had entered the earth through a volcano in Iceland and exited through a volcano near southern Italy!

Our return trip home was by sea and by rail. It went pleasantly. By the ninth of October, we had reached Hamburg. There, we let the world know of our great adventure. True, we had not penetrated to the core of the earth, as Arne Saknussemm had. But we had gone deeper than any other explorer. My uncle became famous, and I with him.

Hans, however, was eager to get back to his home in Iceland. The professor and I rode with Hans to a nearby port. He promptly booked passage on a ship that was leaving for Iceland in half an hour.

My uncle and I watched our loyal guide and close friend walk down the gangway. Then Hans turned around and rushed back. He shook our hands one final time. I closed my hand over his and said, ''Thank you, dear friend, for saving my life. I shall miss you.''

Hans hurried down the gangway as it was about to be lifted away. Then the ship moved out to sea. Hans waved to us from the railing, and we waved back to him.

We watched the ship until it became a dot on the horizon. As I stared out over the water, I wondered if any of us would ever forget our incredible journey.